For Jill, of course
—D.P.

Cataloging-in-Publication Data has been applied for and may be obtained from the Library of Congress.

This book was painted in gouache.

ISBN 978-1-4197-5194-3

Published in 2022 by Abrams Books for Young Readers, an imprint of ABRAMS. All rights reserved. No portion of this book may be reproduced, stored in a retrieval system, or transmitted in any form or by any means, mechanical, electronic, photocopying, recording, or otherwise, without written permission from the publisher.

Printed and bound in China
10 9 8 7 6 5 4 3 2 1

Text © 2022
Daniel Pinkwater

Illustrations © 2022
Aaron Renier

Book design by
Heather Kelly

ABRAMS The Art of Books
195 Broadway, New York, NY 10007
abramsbooks.com

Abrams® is a registered trademark of Harry N. Abrams, Inc.

To Grae
with love,
—A.R.

ABRAMS BOOKS FOR YOUNG READERS · NEW YORK

Jessica

Kat Hats

BY DANIEL PINKWATER

Illustrations BY AARON RENIER

Matt Katz is the president of Kat Hats Incorporated,

a company in the old city of Pretzelburg.

Kat Hats Incorporated
does not make little
hats for cats to wear.

That would be adorable,
but it is not the business of
Matt Katz and his company.

Neither is a Kat Hat a hat for humans to wear, which represents or resembles a cat. This would be delightful and also fashionable—

but what Kat Hats Incorporated produces in the old Catworks in Pretzelburg are specially-trained cats. It is a cat trainery.

The Kat Hat itself is a cat, specially selected for unusual furriness and warmth.

Such a cat is patiently taught to arrange itself on the head of a person as a living headpiece.

And Matt Katz is the foremost cat trainer in the world.

These cats are not sold, but rented to mountain climbers, adventurers, Arctic explorers,

and people living in Chicago.

I hear a **flute.**

I hear low sounds.
I hear **thunder.**

I hear a cow moo.

I hear happy sounds.
I hear laughing.

I hear music.

I hear many sounds.

It is well known that 90 percent of body heat is lost through the top of the head,

so if one's head is warm,
one will remain warm all over,
and could even visit the North Pole in
summer pajamas and remain comfortable.

Matt Katz has a wife,
Glamorella,

who is famous for her peach
and apricot pretzels,

and a son,
Pocketmouse,
and a daughter,
Lambkin.

Like a member
of the family is
Thermal Herman
6⅞ths,

the pride and
joy of Kat Hats,
and the
warmest cat
ever known.

Thermal Herman 6⅞ths
was visiting the family.

He had recently returned from Nepal, where he warmed the head of the head of a mountaineering expedition.

Thermal Herman 6⅞ths brought back harmonicas for the entire family. After a delicious pretzel casserole, the Katzes and the cat sat around the stove and played classical music on their new harmonicas.

There was a knock upon the door.

"Who can it be?" asked Glamorella Katz.

"It is Old Thirdbeard!" shouted Lambkin and Pocketmouse.

Old Thirdbeard was so called because in his youth, he grew two other beards, which he now kept in his dresser drawer and wore on holidays. Thirdbeard was wise and everyone loved him.

Thirdbeard lived in a small cabin of clay and wattles made with Chickarina the witch.

Chickarina was quite a small witch, known to the inhabitants of Pretzelburg. She was a nice witch who did no harm.

And she was the mommy of Thirdbeard.

"I am sorry to interrupt
your musical evening,"
Old Thirdbeard said.
"But I fear my mommy,
Chickarina the witch,
may be in trouble."

MISSING
MY
MOMMY

"What sort of trouble do
you fear Chickarina is in?"
Matt Katz asked Thirdbeard.

"The last time I saw her, she had an extra-large jumbo frozen fruitsicle, blueberry and avocado flavor," Old Thirdbeard said.

"She was licking and sucking on it like there was no tomorrow while walking up the pointy mountain known as the Witch's Spitz."

The Katz family looked out the window at the magnificent peak.
"Ahhh!" they all said, appreciating its beauty.

Thirdbeard
continued, "After
she was out of sight,
I remembered that my
mommy often gets an ice cream
headache or brain freeze when
she eats very cold things.

She has not come back, and I am afraid she is somewhere up on the Witch's Spitz with a frozen brain."

"Was she wearing her witch's hat when last seen?" Matt Katz asked Thirdbeard.

"She was not," Thirdbeard said.

Matt Katz met the eyes of Thermal Herman 6⅞ths.

"You know what to do," Matt Katz said.

"Mrowr," said Thermal Herman 6⅞ths,

and dashed out into the night.

Climbing paw over paw would be too slow.

The great cat had to find a way to get up high in a hurry.

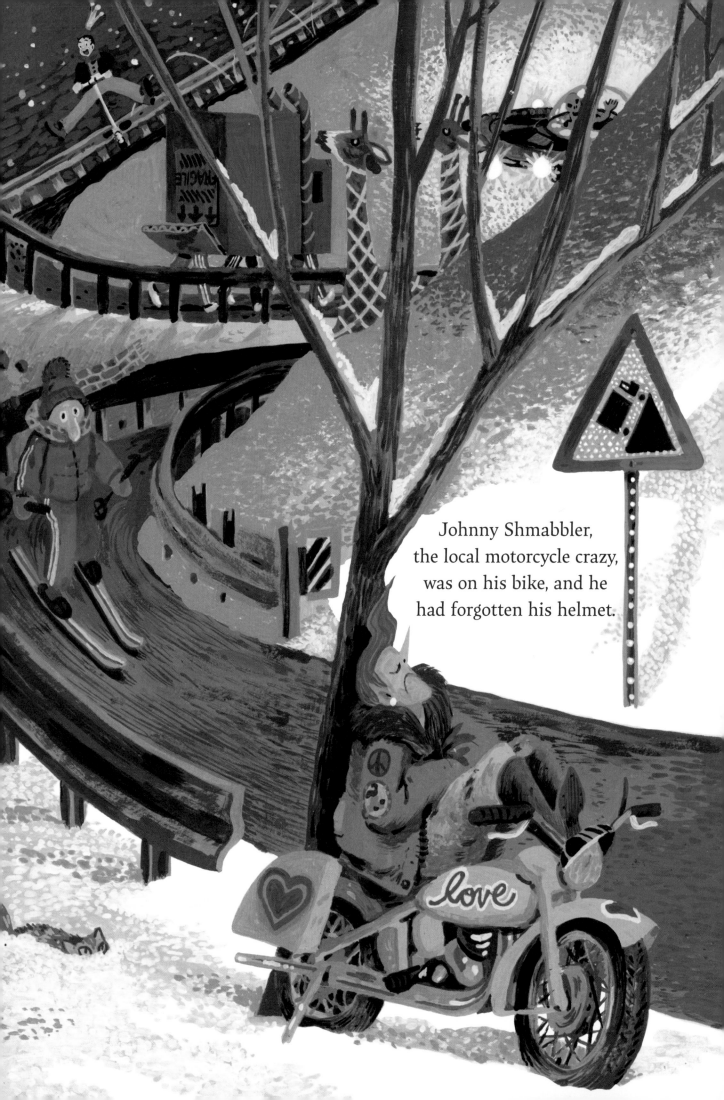

Johnny Shmabbler, the local motorcycle crazy, was on his bike, and he had forgotten his helmet.

Thermal Herman 6⅞ths made his move. He plopped onto Johnny's head, held onto his ears, and waited. He did not have to wait long.

Johnny zoomed up the slope,

going faster and faster,

WATCH FOR ROCK

and crashed into a big rock

about halfway up the mountain.

This had happened before. Several of Johnny's wrecked motorcycles were lying here and there.

Sadly, the cat got a nasty bump on his rump, but he had no time to think about that. The frozen-brained Chickarina was somewhere up the mountain.

There was still a distance to go, and the cat needed some luck.

Here came some luck.

It was a moose, and this moose was
using his antlers as a hat rack.

This was not unusual,
as lots of moose do it.

It was kitten's play for Thermal Herman 6⅞ths to fashion himself into a handsome fedora,

fit in among the moose's other hats, and dangle from an antler point.

The moose was not as fast as Johnny on a motorcycle, but he took long steps up the mountain,

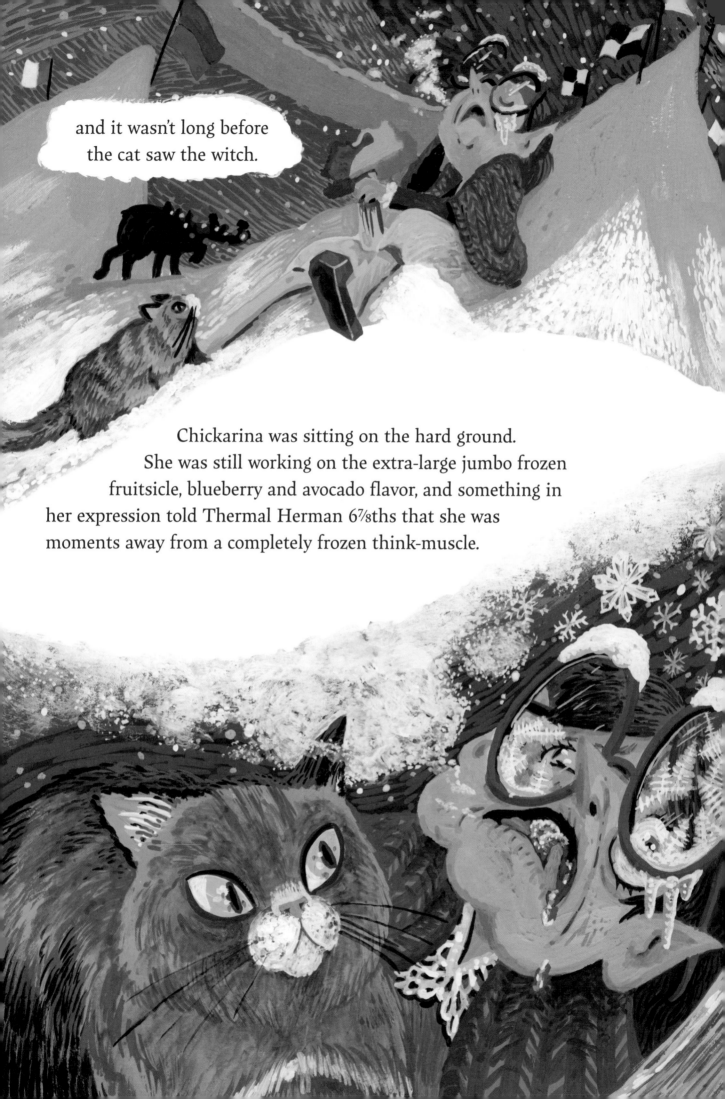

and it wasn't long before the cat saw the witch.

Chickarina was sitting on the hard ground. She was still working on the extra-large jumbo frozen fruitsicle, blueberry and avocado flavor, and something in her expression told Thermal Herman 6⅞ths that she was moments away from a completely frozen think-muscle.

Thermal Herman 6⅞ths deftly assembled himself into the perfect likeness of a stylish witch-lid and stood by.

He did not have to wait long.

"Now where did I put my hat?" Chickarina mused to herself. "Ah! There it is, and it seems so much warmer and nicer than usual."

"Thermal Herman 6⅞ths!" everyone shouted.

"Thermal Herman 6⅞ths has saved her!"

"Did you save me some leftover pretzel casserole?" Chickarina the witch asked.

"We certainly did," Thirdbeard said.

"Let us serenade our brave Thermal Herman 6⅞ths, and also Thirdbeard and his mommy, Chickarina the witch," Matt Katz said.

The Katz family took out their brand-new harmonicas.

"The piece we will play is 'Twinkle, Twinkle, Little Star' by Mister Wolfgang A. Mozart. One, two, three, begin!"

Kat Hats